MY FIRST NUMBERS

Address all inquiries to:
Barron's Educational Series, Inc.
250 Wireless Boulevard
Hauppauge, New York 11788

Library of Congress Catalog Card No. 94-1090

International Standard Book No. 0-8120-6314-7

Printed in France
4567 9655 987654321

MY FIRST NUMBERS

Françoise Audry-Iljic   Thierry Courtin
Adapted by Judith Herbst

BARRON'S

THE STORY OF LEARNING

Well before learning to read, children are enthusiastic about numbers. At first numbers are nothing more than words without meaning. Then, little by little, the significance of numbers is planted in their brain. Knowing how to count is not just reciting the numbers, it is being able to count objects, to associate the numbers with their corresponding quantities. We forget that numbers have no visual quality as do colors; numbers are somewhat abstract. The child must at some point go beyond "1, 2, and many more" to "1, 2, 3, 4, 5, . . ." and then to understanding that 3 bears, 3 bowls, 3 spoons, have something in common that allows them to be categorized and makes them correspond to 3 fingers of the hand, 3 billiard balls, in short, that 3 is always 3.

Up to 5, numbers can be understood universally, without counting; they refer to the child's primary experience: 2, as the child's two hands; 3, as the mother-father-child trio; 4, visualized by four animal paws in motion; 5, which are the number of fingers on each hand. Beyond this, the number can no longer be identified at a glance, except for a particular grouping, such as the hands or a pair of dice: 6 is $5 + 1$ or $3 + 3$, or even 3×2 or 2×3. At this point, the child arrives instinctively at the very basis of arithmetic, at the rudiments of addition, division, and multiplication. Subtraction is more difficult because it is the loss or taking away of something, just like the little child who loses his apples one by one on the way home; it involves backward movement.

A special place has been reserved for 0, which gives meaning to all the other numbers; it lets the child erase everything to begin again. Having reached 10, the child is ready to take on another group of ten. For the moment, though, nothing is gained by counting further and nothing is lost by taking one's time.

Counting, at this age, means sharing cherries with your teddy bears, it is counting and recounting, again and again, for the pleasure of it, to determine the contents of a box of treasures. Counting is truly child's play!

Big round **zero**, filled with air,
shows us when there's nothing there.

It doesn't add, it can't subtract.
Still, we need it, that's a fact!

1 is like a small umbrella,
standing stiff and tall.

Wow! It's fun to count to **one**.
Just raise your thumb, that's all!

2, your neck is gently curving;
like a swan, you float with grace.

Two can help you count your socks
and put them in the proper place.

3 is like a set of shelves to hold
my toys and stuff.

Mom, Dad, and I make **three**,
and that is just enough.

4 makes a sail for my toy boat—
hop aboard and away we'll float.

Who's on all **fours**, creeping like that,
making believe that he's a cat?

Counting to **5** is easy as pie, just count the fingers on your hand . . .
4 fingers, **1** thumb—isn't that grand?

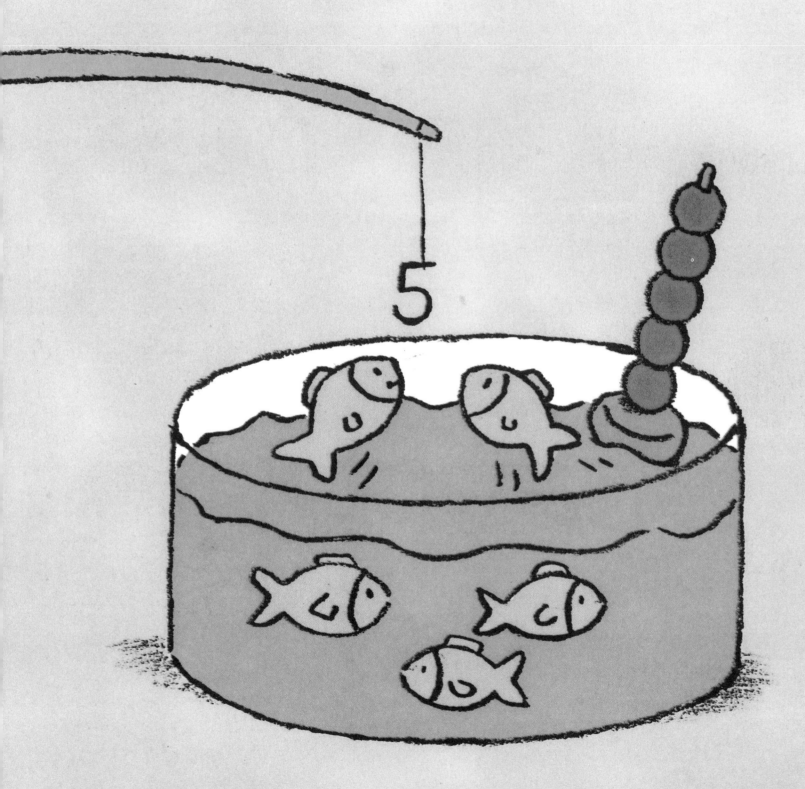

Five will make a dandy hook to fish for numbers in this book.
I think I've got a bite! Oh, look!

6 can do some yo-yo tricks.
It winds around and forms a loop.

What is this group, this little troop, these fellows from a chicken coop?
Five on this side, **one** on the other,
that makes **six** chicks looking for their mother.

7 has been pushed aside; it leans but doesn't fall.

You have seen the **seven** dwarfs, but can you name them all?

I can race my cars on **8**. As a speedway, gee! It's great!
Round and round they navigate, never ever driving straight.

Would you like to see my cars? **Four** are green and **four** are red.
I've got **eight** cars I can race, but I'll just park them here instead.

9 is like a cowboy lasso, absolutely genuine.
If I were a number cowboy, I could rope the number **9**.

I love to play on checkerboards; I hop around the squares.
Five are black and **four** are white. I hop the squares from left to right.
Back and forth I hop, hop, hop, and when I've touched all **nine**, I stop!

10 little fingers standing tall,
to count to **10** just count them all.

But when I want to write a **ten**, I call the **zero** back again,
and roll it right next to the **one**. Numbers are a lot of fun!

10 little bowling pins all in rows . . .
what will happen, do you suppose?

Crash! go the pins as the ball knocks them flat.
Every last one, imagine that! **Zero** pins left in nice, neat rows…
how many fell, do you suppose?

Ten little bowling pins marching away,
back to the closet for the rest of the day.

1 is first and 10 is last,
10 little bowling pins, marching past.

How many teddy bears in this bunch?
Let's count them up and serve them lunch.

1 big bear who looks so wise, **1** bear who is a medium size,
1 small bear with shining eyes—**1**, **2**, **3** bears hungry for pies.

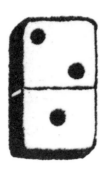

All **3** bears are ready to eat, hoping for something tasty and sweet.
Will they get their wishes? First they need some dishes.

3 bowls empty, waiting for stew,
Big bowl, medium bowl, small bowl, too.

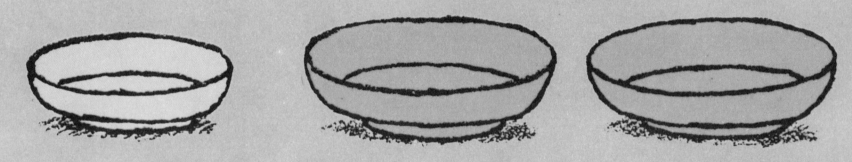

3 plates empty, waiting for cheese,
Small plate, big plates (**2** of these).

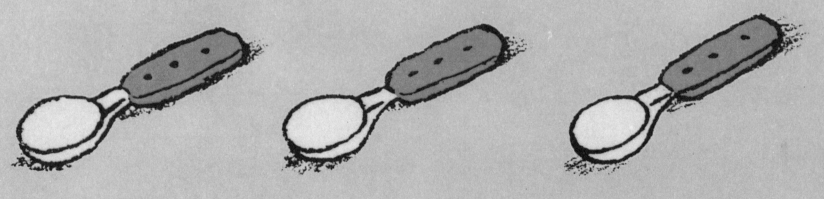

3 spoons empty, waiting for soup,
Each **1** has the same size scoop.

Cherries on the kitchen table—I can climb and reach them all.
Will you help me count the cherries? Gosh! I hope that I don't fall!

Look at me, I'm acting silly, wearing cherries on my head.
2 on one ear, **2** on the other, **4** big cherries, juicy and red.
But fruit is not for wearing, it's for snacking on and sharing…

The bears are back, their lips go smack!
They're hungry for a cherry snack.
Each bear gets the same amount. How many cherries do you count?
2 for you, and **2** for you, and **2** more for the big bear, too.

Gone are the cherries, **2** by **2**. How many were there? Here's a clue:
6 little stems were left behind. **6** little pits are all we find.

But if I plan to have a party, cherries simply will not do.
They're much too small to feed us all, so how about cake? With frosting, too!
1 big cake with lots of cream, fluffy, puffy birthday dream.

We'll gather 'round, I'll make a wish, and blow the candles out.
I'll get them all with **1** big POOF! "Hooray!" the bears will shout.
And if you count along the way, you'll know how old I am today.

Are all these presents just for me?
How many presents do you see?

If you stack them **1** by **1**,
Counting can be lots of fun!

2 hands are handy, perfectly dandy,
so nice for loosening bows that are tied.
10 fingers wiggle, waggle, and jiggle, to unwrap the wrapping and see what's inside.

Little helpers, they're my fingers,
always there to do the job.
5 on **1** hand hold a basket,
5 to help me turn a knob.

Want to know what makes me smile? Apples in a little pile.
1, **2**, **3**, **4**, **5**, I see, **5** fresh apples from the tree,
in my basket made of wood. Mmmm! I bet they sure taste good.

I thought I had a real tight grip when I began to hop and skip.
But, oh! My basket bounced about, and knocked **1** apple up and out.
Now there are only **4** you see, but **4** are good enough for me.

I stooped to pick a small bouquet, and **1** more apple rolled away.
I guess it was an accident, my basket tilted, out it went.
Now there are only **3** you see, but **3** are good enough for me.

I ran as fast as I could go, my basket teetered to and fro.
The apples bumped and jumped around, and **1** came tumbling to the ground.
Now there are only **2** you see, but **2** are good enough for me.

Oh, my gosh! I really slipped! My basket fell and nearly tipped.
I bet you know what happened then—I lost an apple once again.
Now there's only **1** you see, but **1** is good enough for me.

No more apples in my basket, nothing left to tilt and spill.
1 last apple, should I eat it? Should I? Should I?
Yes, I will!

Look at me, I'll count to **10**, and then I'll count to **10** again.
It's easy when you know the way, and you can smile and proudly say,
"Hooray for me! I'm really swell!" "I learned my numbers very well!"

1 green pencil, **1** blue ball,
2 brown chestnuts, and that's not all . . .
3 sweet candies I can share, **4** big buttons lying there,
in a box that's blue and red, tucked away beneath my bed.

Imprimé par AUBIN IMPRIMEUR - Relié par BRUN